AF426584

THEWIZARDCOW

The Detective Between Worlds

A Journal of Hidden Keys and Liminal Spaces

Contents

(Entry #1: Something Beyond the Old Building)

They say a good detective never ignores their gut. Mine had been unsettled for days, churning at the edges of this missing person case like an animal circling a trap. I remember the rain on my collar and the dull hum of traffic when I stepped off the curb that evening, heading toward the old building where my lead had pointed me. The city's neon signs wavered in puddles, turning each reflection into a lurid painting beneath my feet. It was late, a time when my side of town always carried a hush. I think it was nearly midnight, give or take an hour. I'd stopped checking my watch, too annoyed at the lack of progress.

The missing person—Marina Kemp—had been last seen around here. Her brother, a worried sort with tired eyes, had hired me days ago. The police had nothing. The trail was cold. But I kept hearing rumors: neighbors saw her enter this boarded-up building, some old construction abandoned halfway through completion, then never saw her come out. It sounded improbable. But people vanish in cities like this all the time, and I've learned not to dismiss even the wildest hints.

The front door was easy enough to breach; its chain had long since rusted and snapped with a tug. Inside, I expected dust, maybe rotting wood, the smell of damp plaster. I did find those things. But I also found something else: silence, absolute and thick. No creak of settling beams, no distant hum of ventilation. Just my own breathing and the scrape of my shoes on the uneven floor.

I fished out my flashlight and swept its beam along the walls. I saw graffitied symbols I didn't recognize—wide loops, crossed lines—and a half-finished staircase leading to what looked like a corridor. The building's blueprint made no sense. From the outside, it looked like a three-story commercial property left to rot. Inside, the angles didn't match. Hallways extended where I thought the building's exterior wall should be. Doors led to empty rooms, some big enough to be ballrooms, some too narrow for me to squeeze through. It was unsettling, but I pressed on. I'd seen plenty of strange floor plans in my time.

I tried calling out Marina's name, once or twice, just in case. My voice fell flat. I followed footprints in the dust—boot marks as if someone before me had been pacing around. They led me down a corridor lit only by my flashlight's faint glow. Each step I took felt longer than the last as if the floor was stretching beneath my feet. At one point, I turned to see how far I'd gone. The entrance door was gone, just darkness behind me. The sound of distant dripping water echoed from somewhere ahead.

I told myself to stay calm. Maybe I took a wrong turn. Maybe it was just the odd shape of the place. I carefully retraced my steps—or tried to. Every turn led to another corridor, another empty room, each disturbingly similar. At first, I placed my hand on the damp, peeling wallpaper, leaving a faint smudge to mark my path. When I circled back to check it, the mark was gone.

I might have been down there for twenty minutes or two hours—time felt strange. Eventually, I found a door with a broken hinge that I was sure I hadn't passed before. It stood slightly ajar, and a pale, flickering light seeped from within. I approached, pushing it open with my shoulder. The space beyond was... wrong. It looked like a hallway, but longer than anything that could fit in that building. As I shone my flashlight down it, I realized I couldn't see the end. The light just faded into gloom.

Something about that corridor made my stomach twist. It smelled stale, like old carpet and dead air. My gut told me to turn back, to try and smash through a window, anything. But I'd seen no windows, no obvious exits. And the door I had just come through was now closed—when I spun around to reopen it, it was gone. No sign a door had ever been there. The wall was seamless, and my mark of dust was nowhere to be found.

I shouted then, a short, sharp curse that echoed oddly. My nerves rattled. I didn't know what was happening, and I sure as hell didn't like it. But I refused to panic. I have been in tight corners before—though never this bizarre—and I knew that panic gets you nowhere. I decided to walk forward, keeping careful track of each step, counting them under my breath. If I had to, I'd follow that corridor until I found some kind of landmark or branching path.

As I moved, the flashlight began to flicker. Its beam guttered, and for a moment, I stood in near darkness, hearing my breathing louder than ever. Then it steadied. In that brief flicker, I thought I saw something ahead, a shape moving at the edge of my vision. I called out, hoping it was Marina or at least someone who could explain this madness. No answer came.

Step by step, I continued forward, legs heavy with tension. The corridor never seemed to end. I passed occasional doorways, all sealed, their knobs unwilling to turn. I marked the walls again, but every time I checked, the marks were gone. It began to dawn on me that this place, wherever it was, did not follow the normal rules of space and time.

After what felt like an eternity, I paused to gather my thoughts. I took out my notebook from my coat's inner pocket—the same one I use for case notes—and began writing this down. Partly to keep track of events, and partly to ensure my sanity. I'm not sure how much time I'll spend trapped in here, but I want a record—something to prove to myself that I'm still me, that I haven't lost it entirely.

I wrote down today's date at the top of the page—if the date even matters here. I detailed how I followed the missing person's trail. How did I end up in this impossible place? It's an ordinary notebook, with lined pages, and blue ink. The scratching of the pen against paper felt comforting, a reminder of normalcy.

As I stand here, leaning against a faded wall, I have to accept the situation. The city I know is gone. The building's entrance is gone. I am somewhere else. Somewhere in-between, perhaps. I can't deny what I've seen: corridors that don't end, disappearing doors, a silence that feels alive. Whatever this place is, I must treat it like a puzzle, a problem to solve. I'm a detective, after all—that's what I do. I find answers.

I don't know where Marina is, or if she's even here. I don't know if I'm the only one trapped in this dimension of endless halls. But I do know one thing: I have to keep moving forward. Maybe this corridor leads somewhere. Maybe I'll meet someone—or something—willing to talk. Maybe I'll find a clue, a key, a path home. One step at a time.

For now, I'll end this entry. There's no turning back. I'm going to keep writing as I go, keep my thoughts anchored on these pages. It's my lifeline to who I am and where I've come from. If I survive this, I'll need the record. If I don't... well, at least these words will remain, assuming anyone ever finds them.

(Entry #2: A Labyrinth of Dim Light)

I don't know how much time passed between my last note and this moment. My watch face has started to play tricks on me—one minute, the hands crawl forward as normal; the next, they stall or jump ahead unexpectedly. But time aside, I'm still here, in these hallways that loop and bend in ways I can't understand. The silence presses in, heavier than before. Even my footsteps sound dull as if absorbed by the floor.

After finishing the previous entry, I resumed my slow exploration. I tried to count my steps to maintain some sense of measure. One hundred steps, then two hundred. Occasionally I'd stop and place a hand against the wall, feeling the gentle give of the wallpaper under my fingers, the faint grit of plaster behind it. Sometimes I thought I could sense a subtle vibration, like a distant hum with no clear source. Could it be wiring in the walls? Some hidden machinery? Or is it just my mind playing tricks?

My attempts at navigation keep failing. Every so often, I choose a direction at random—left or right at a branching hall—only to find myself in what feels like the same place. The overhead lighting is inconsistent; some stretches are well-lit, others barely illuminated by a distant glow. I'm forced to rely on my flashlight in those darker reaches. The battery still seems strong, but I worry. What if it fails me?

I tried marking the walls again. This time I tore a corner from a page in my notebook and pressed it into a small crack where the wallpaper peeled. When I returned after a short loop of walking, the scrap of paper was gone. It's as if the space rearranges itself whenever I'm not looking. Once, I nearly convinced myself the hallway shifted the instant I blinked. My mind resists that conclusion—it's too absurd—but I have little else to go on.

Then there was the sound of steps. I'm certain I heard them. Muffled at first, as though someone walked behind the walls. I called out, my voice echoing back, hollow and distorted. For a few heartbeats, I thought I heard a response—just a whisper, too faint to decipher. I followed it, pressing my ear to the wall where it sounded strongest. Silence. I waited a long moment, knuckles against the dusty surface, but there was nothing more.

I walked on, turning corners until I found a stretch of hallway where a soft light flickered. It looked almost like a candle flame, though I found no candle. Instead, I spotted a figure at a distance—a vague silhouette leaning around a doorway. My heart skipped. If this was Marina, or anyone human, maybe I could get answers. I raised my voice, careful and calm, introducing myself, and asking if they were okay. The figure didn't respond. Instead, it drew back out of sight.

I hurried forward, each footstep echoing. When I reached the spot, I found no one. Just another dead end with wallpaper peeling at the corners. No footprints, no sign of disturbance. But something had to have been there, right? I'm not losing it. I can't afford to.

I moved on, and that's when I noticed a scrap of paper on the floor. It wasn't mine. The color was off-white, a bit thicker. I knelt and picked it up. On it, written in a shaky hand, were the words: "Follow the messenger." Nothing else. No signature. The ink looked fresh. I pocketed it, questions swirling. What messenger? Could it mean the figure I just saw?

With no other lead, I continued searching. Gradually, the hallway widened into a small foyer-like space—at least something larger than a corridor. The ceiling arched here, and old chairs lined one side, their fabric worn and muted. It felt like a waiting area if that makes any sense in a place like this. I took a seat, relieved to rest my legs, and shone my flashlight around. Each doorway out of this space looked identical, except for one with a faint symbol scratched into the wood near the handle. It resembled a spiral with a slash through it. Perhaps a clue?

I decided to try that door first. It opened easily, revealing not another corridor, but a narrow staircase descending into semi-darkness. The air changed—cooler, a bit musty. Quiet as I could, I descended. My footsteps made muffled thuds on the steps. Halfway down, I heard a soft voice, like someone humming a tune without melody. I froze and listened. The humming continued, distant and gentle. Maybe I should've called out, but part of me hesitated, fearing that whatever hummed wouldn't be human.

At the bottom of the stairs, I found a small room. Its walls were lined with shelves holding objects I couldn't identify—strange boxes, twisted metal frames, a piece of cloth shimmering oddly in my flashlight beam. In the center stood a tall figure draped in something like a hooded cloak. I couldn't see a face, just a vague outline of where a head should be. The humming ceased.

"Are you the messenger?" I asked quietly.

The figure nodded—or seemed to. Its outline flickered as if seen through old glass. Then it raised an arm, long and thin, pointing to a ledger that lay open on a stool by the shelf. Nervous but curious, I approached the ledger. Its pages turned by themselves with a soft papery hush until they stopped at a drawing—a simple map. Or at least, it looked like a map: corridors drawn as lines, rooms as boxes, and a small mark circled in red.

I leaned in, squinting. "What is this?"

The figure's voice emerged in a whisper—genderless, gentle. "The path you must walk. One who fell between worlds must earn a way back. A role awaits you. Take up the ledger, solve what's lost, and keys shall guide you home."

It sounded unbelievable, but what choice did I have? I reached out, touching the ledger. It felt strangely warm. "Solve what's lost," I repeated. "What does that mean? Who are you?"

The figure didn't answer. Instead, it pressed a thin object into my hand. A slip of paper with strange symbols. Then it receded into the shadows, the edges of its form dissolving into the gloom. I shouted, stumbling forward, but found only empty shelves and silent walls. The figure—this so-called messenger—vanished entirely.

I ran my thumb over the slip of paper, trying to make sense of the symbols. There were a few lines and spirals, something that might be coordinates or directions. I flipped it over—blank on the other side.

"Must earn a way back," I muttered, feeling a chill that had nothing to do with the air. I've dealt with cryptic clues before, but never like this. The messenger had spoken of keys and solving something lost. Was I now tasked with some kind of inter-dimensional detective work? The very idea sounded absurd.

Yet what else was I to do? I'm trapped. There's a logic here, twisted as it is. If I was given instructions and a map, maybe there's a purpose. If I find what the messenger wants me to find, maybe I can escape. Returning home—just the thought steadied me. My old life, my apartment, the coffee shop on the corner. I'm not ready to give that up.

I tucked the ledger under my arm, pocketed the slip of paper, and climbed back up the stairs. The foyer awaited me, unchanged. I examined the ledger again. Its pages now held words I didn't remember writing. Names, partial descriptions, fragments of cases: "A traveler lost in shifting mirrors," "A device stolen from stabilizing thresholds," "An artifact hidden in a place with no true floors." These riddles made little sense, yet I felt certain they pertained to tasks I'd have to complete.

Before I could think further, I heard quiet footsteps in the corridor beyond the foyer. Maybe the messenger was still near, or perhaps someone else, another trapped soul. I followed the sound, half-expecting it to vanish again. To my surprise, I glimpsed a second figure—a receptionist-like silhouette standing behind what looked like a counter that hadn't been there a moment ago. As I approached, the figure handed me a thin folder without a word. Inside were instructions, more direct this time: "Case #1: Missing traveler. Find them beyond the reflecting halls."

I looked up to question the figure, but it was gone, and so was the counter.

Everything here is slippery, shifting. I feel like a piece on a chessboard being nudged from square to square by invisible hands. Still, a direction is better than aimless wandering. I have a place to start: the reflecting halls. Maybe I can find this missing traveler, earn whatever key they spoke of, and take one step closer to home.

I will write as often as I can. Every word keeps me tethered to reality. This place wants to confuse me, wants me to lose myself in looping corridors and vanish like Marina. I refuse. I'm a detective, and I will find my way out—no matter how strange these riddles become.

(Entry #3: A Place of Shifting Reflections)

I've begun to think of these corridors as a kind of puzzle box, each space a clue waiting to be deciphered. After the encounter with the messenger and the whispered commission, I set out with fresh determination. The first case, as dictated by that bizarre folder, is to find a missing traveler in what it called the "reflecting halls."

Guided by the slip of paper and the ledger, I searched for any hint of mirrored surfaces. Eventually, a series of corridors led me somewhere markedly different. The air became cooler, and the usual pattern of wallpaper gave way to something shinier, more polished. Light behaved strangely there, stretching and bending as if passing through a prism. I turned a corner and stumbled into a hallway lined with panels of polished metal—or possibly glass—each reflecting my image in distorted forms.

The moment I stepped into this space, I felt watched. My flashlight beam danced across panels that made my reflection tall, then short, then impossibly thin. After a few paces, I realized the floor itself had a faint shimmer, as though coated with a reflective varnish. A misplaced step caused my footfall to echo twice as if the sound bounced back at me. I flicked off my flashlight, testing how darkness affected this place. Dim overhead lights—if you could call them that—provided enough glow to see, and in their gentle illumination, my shape multiplied a thousand times in the mirrored surfaces.

"Marina?" I tried, but my voice came back to me warped, overlapping like a chorus of strangers imitating me. No human replies just echoes. Still, I'm here for a traveler, not necessarily Marina. Perhaps this missing person has left some trace.

I walked slowly, scanning every surface. Some panels seemed loose as if they were thin sheets hung over hollow frames. Others felt solid and cold. I tried pressing my palm against one; it was smooth and chilled, giving back no vibration. But the next panel I touched hummed quietly, sending a faint tingle up my arm. I leaned closer and thought I saw a faint outline of a figure on the other side—a silhouette not matching my own.

I whispered, "Hello?" and received a soft, uncertain murmur in return. The silhouette moved, drifting across the panel as if walking behind a veil of silver. I rapped my knuckles on the surface and the figure paused. Then, with a trembling voice, it said, "Who's there?" The voice was muffled as if speaking through thick glass.

My heart skipped. "I'm a detective," I said, feeling slightly ridiculous announcing my profession to someone trapped behind a mirror. "I'm here to help. Are you the missing traveler?"

Silence for a moment, then: "I don't know what they call me. I'm lost. I came here through... well, I'm not sure how I came here. Please—can you get me out? I've tried everything. The reflections won't let me pass."

I pressed my ear closer. "Reflections won't let you pass?"

The figure sounded tired, on the verge of despair. "If I step forward, I hit a barrier. I see corridors stretching behind me, but they're never the right ones. My reflection doesn't match my movements exactly. Sometimes it lags or moves ahead. I'm trapped behind a looking-glass world."

I remembered the ledger's cryptic notes. I pulled it out and flipped through its pages, which seemed to shift and rewrite themselves when I wasn't looking. One line, in particular, caught my eye: "To free the traveler, realign the corridor by extinguishing your light and counting to ten." It sounded nonsensical, but I had nothing else to go on.

I leaned toward the panel. "I'm going to try something. Stay calm."

I switched off my flashlight completely. The darkness intensified, making the mirrored surfaces fade into silhouettes. I counted slowly under my breath: one, two, three... at five, I heard a distant scraping, as if the halls were adjusting themselves. At eight, a soft click echoed. At ten, I switched my flashlight back on.

The corridor looked different now. The reflections had shifted. Instead of endless variations of me, I saw a more uniform reflection—just one version of myself, slightly off-center. I approached the panel where I'd spoken to the traveler and found that it now reflected a slender person wearing a tattered coat, a real individual behind the glass. They stared at me with wide, hopeful eyes.

"Try stepping through," I said. I pressed my hand against the panel. This time, it felt softer, more like a membrane than hard glass. On the other side, the traveler did the same. Our fingertips aligned. I pushed gently, and the traveler's hand met mine. With a soft, watery distortion, they slipped through. One second, they were behind the surface; the next, they stood beside me, shaking, breathing heavily.

They looked human—haunted eyes, dust-smudged faces, and a trembling smile. "I—I'm free?" they whispered, voice quavering.

I nodded, trying not to show my relief. "Seems like it. Are you hurt?"

They shook their head. "Only confused, tired. I've been stuck here for what felt like days, maybe longer. Everything kept repeating. My reflection trapped me, echoing my every move but never letting me exit."

I took a moment to scan the corridor. The distortion was gone; each panel now showed a consistent reflection. The dim light reflected my tired face at me, unchanged. "I'm supposed to bring you back," I said, though I wasn't entirely sure what 'back' meant in this context.

The traveler looked at me as if I were their savior. Before I could question them further—about who they were, how they ended up here—they began to fade. Not stepping away, not disappearing into the halls, but fading, as if turning to smoke in soft lamplight. I reached out to catch their arm, but my hand passed through space. They vanished without another word.

In the spot where they stood, a small object lay on the floor—a key, fashioned from a dark, glossy material I couldn't identify. It was roughly the length of my thumb and oddly warm to the touch. As I picked it up, the ledger's pages fluttered. A faint whisper drifted through the hall: "One key earned."

I pocketed the key, my heart pounding. So it was true: completing these tasks grants me keys. And keys, they said, would help me open a path home.

I'm not sure if the traveler I rescued was the same missing person I'd set out to find originally, but it seems I'm now working under entirely different rules. I wonder if Marina even matters here, or if she's just another stepping stone in a much larger, stranger puzzle.

With the key in my pocket, I retraced my steps. The reflective corridor looked more stable now, less daunting. Eventually, I found my way back to that foyer-like space—though now it had shifted. The chairs were gone, the archway slightly taller. A door I hadn't noticed before stood ajar, leading into an office-like chamber. Inside, I found a desk and a figure who might have been the receptionist I'd glimpsed earlier, or another being altogether. They took the key from me—just briefly—and placed it into a small pouch. Then, without a word, they nodded and handed it back. It felt heavier somehow, more real.

I left the chamber and found myself back in the strange "office" environment, where corridors lead into uncharted territory. The Chief Inspector—if I can call them that—stood in silhouette at the far end, acknowledging my success with a measured incline of the head. No words were exchanged, yet I understood: two more keys. I need two more keys to negotiate my return.

I'm exhausted but also determined. I've solved one case and freed one lost soul. I have proof that these halls, for all their strangeness, operate by certain rules. And that means I can master them, one puzzle at a time.

Now I'm writing this entry down in a quiet corner near the office's entryway, sitting on a stool that appeared out of nowhere. The ledger rests beside me, its pages blank except for faint impressions of previous clues. I wonder what the next case will be—what impossible rescue or retrieval I'll have to perform. I don't know yet, but I feel a glimmer of purpose. If I keep my head, if I keep recording my thoughts, I might just make it home again.

For now, I'll rest and gather my strength. Keys, corridors, and shifting reflections... I'm in deep. But I'm still a detective, and I still have a job to do.

(Entry #4: Negotiations in the Dimensional Office)

I've rested longer than I intended—though how to measure "longer" here is beyond me. Time has no anchor. My watch, once reliable, now seems as much a prop as my flashlight. It's stuck at the same time I first stepped through that impossible threshold. Maybe my old life is paused out there. Maybe I'll return and find only seconds have passed. Or maybe years will have slipped by. I can't let that thought paralyze me. Instead, I focus on the here and now: the next step, the next case, the next key.

I'm back in what I've come to call the Dimensional Office. It's difficult to describe this place. It feels like a hub or a nexus. Corridors radiate from a central chamber that looks half like a waiting room, and half like a gallery of curiosities. Furniture rearranges itself subtly whenever I glance away—tables shift a few inches, chairs change their upholstery, and doorways tilt at angles that strain the eye. And always, there's that hush. Not silence, exactly, but a subdued energy, like the muffled murmur of a distant crowd just beyond a wall.

The Chief Inspector (or that's what I've named them in my mind) emerges again, a figure more silhouette than a person. They move without footsteps, their form stable yet indistinct as if made of dense shadow. I see no face, but I sense eyes on me. They regard me as if evaluating my worth. I want to ask them everything: Who are you? What is this place? Why me? But I suspect I wouldn't get straight answers. This realm thrives on obscurity and subtle hints.

Instead, I speak calmly. "I have one key. You said I need more."

A pause, then a slight inclination of their head. With one hand—if you can call that shape a hand—they indicate a low table that wasn't there moments ago. On it sits a slim folder, similar to the last one. I approach and open it. Inside are a few lines of neat, blocky text:

Case #2: A stabilizing device has been stolen from an anchor point. Without it, certain thresholds will collapse, and corridors will devour themselves. Recover the device and return it here. Only then will a second key form.

The text seems to shimmer, and when I blink, it's gone. Just a blank page remains. I close the folder, tuck it under my arm, and turn to the Inspector. "You want me to find this device," I say. "Another puzzle, another strange dimension?"

They tilt their head, almost in sympathy, almost mocking. The ledger at my hip warms, and I sense new hints waiting in its pages. I'm learning that here, instructions manifest in objects, rooms, and whispers. Negotiation seems futile. I'm a detective, yes—but I'm also a pawn, being moved through a cosmic scavenger hunt.

For a moment, anger flares. "Tell me something," I say, struggling to keep my voice steady. "How do I know you'll let me go after three keys? How do I know this isn't just a trap?"

The silhouette doesn't respond with words. Instead, the overhead lighting dims, and a shape flickers at the edge of my vision—like a window to my old apartment. I see my kitchen table, my coffee mug still resting on a newspaper, and sunlight angling through the blinds. It's an illusion, but it stings my heart. When I turn fully, it's gone. A cruel reminder of what I stand to regain if I play by their rules.

I sigh. "Fine. I'll do it." There's no sense pretending I have other options.

The Inspector drifts backward, dissolving into a corridor. I'm left alone, holding the folder. Now I notice others in the "waiting room"—odd entities with concealed faces, half-formed bodies, or features that feel out of place. One paces nervously, though its feet make no sound. Another sits hunched, muttering nonsense phrases that make my teeth ache. Perhaps they are also waiting for help or guidance. The idea that I'm not the only "case worker" here unsettles me, but I have no time for them now.

I open the ledger and find a map sketched in thin, spidery lines. It shows looping hallways and a note: "The device lies in chambers that smell of damp cloth and stale air. Seek rooms that repeat themselves endlessly. Listen for the hum of machinery beneath the quiet."

I set off, choosing one of the corridors leading out of the office. It narrows quickly, the floor beneath my shoes changing from hard tile to spongy carpet. With every step, I think of home: the comforting noise of my city, the reassuring click of door locks, the smell of fresh coffee. I must keep these memories alive. If I lose them, I fear I might become like the nameless beings drifting through these halls.

My flashlight beam wavers against walls that all look the same: muted tones, and worn patterns. After a few turns, I realize I'm deep in a place where every room tries to impersonate the last. The air is stale, carrying a hint of old fabric. The ledger said the device's absence threatens to collapse these thresholds. That suggests the device is crucial to maintaining order.

I can't tell if that's a good thing. If these corridors collapse, would that free me or trap me forever?

Pushing that thought aside, I pause in a T-junction. I close my eyes and listen. My breathing, a distant hiss of static overhead, maybe the hum of an unseen electrical current. Which way to go? The ledger gave me no direct route, just clues.

I pick the left corridor and follow it until I reach a small niche in the wall. Inside is an object—a twisted wire sculpture, meaningless at first glance— yet when I lift it, it emits a faint chime. Suddenly, the corridor shifts. I turn around and find a different hallway than the one I came through. This place can rearrange itself based on interactions. Good to know.

I continue forward, turning corners, leaving small marks of my own: a thread from my coat sleeve knotted around a doorknob, a fingerprint in the dust. Sometimes my marks vanish, but sometimes they don't. I learn to check frequently. Even small consistencies might help me navigate.

After what feels like hours, I come upon a hallway lit by a single flickering lamp. Beneath that lamp, I hear it: a faint mechanical whir, like gears turning behind plaster. I slow down, shining my flashlight into every dark corner. I glimpse a shape hunched over something, a large figure with too-long arms. It fiddles with a metal object. Could that be the stabilizing device?

I dim my flashlight by covering part of the lens with my hand. Quietly, I approach. The figure's back is turned, and as I near, I see it holding a cylindrical apparatus dotted with wires and glowing filaments. It must be what I'm looking for. The device hums softly, and I sense it stabilizing something intangible. Without it, these halls might twist into nothingness.

The figure hears me. It turns a head that shouldn't be able to turn that far. Its face is featureless, its body draped in tattered rags. I say nothing, but the thing hisses softly. I can't tell if it's guarding the device or just examining it. I'll need to be clever.

I rummage quietly in my pocket and pull out the small key I earned earlier. The key warms my palm. When I hold it up, the figure tilts its head, curious. Using this distraction, I edge closer to a corner of the hallway, where I might find a better angle to grab the device. If I can surprise it...

But before I try, I remember the traveler and how I freed them. This place might respond to unusual logic. What if I can trick the creature without confrontation?

I take out the ledger and let its pages fall open. They show me a sequence: shine the flashlight twice, tap the wall three times, and whisper a phrase. It looks absurd, but I trust the ledger now. I do as instructed: I switch the flashlight off, then on, off, and then on again. I tap the plastered wall near my shoulder three times: tap, tap, tap. Then I whisper the phrase that appears on the ledger's page, a half-rhyme that leaves my tongue tingling.

The figure shudders. Its grip on the device loosens. It stands, uncertain, as if disoriented. Taking the chance, I step forward quietly and place a hand on the device. Its surface vibrates gently under my touch. I pull it away, and to my relief, the figure doesn't resist. Instead, it stumbles backward into the shadows, fading like a reflection in a darkened glass.

I have the stabilizing device. It's heavier than it looks and hums softly, warm in my hands. My job now is to return it to the Office, where I hope I'll receive my second key. Then I'll be one step closer to leaving this mad labyrinth behind.

I make my way back—if one can call it that. The corridors rearrange yet again. This time, though, the device's hum guides me. When I take a wrong turn, the hum's pitch changes. It leads me through a series of turns and descents until, at last, I emerge into familiar territory: the Office's central space, chairs, and reception desk are now arranged in calm, symmetrical order.

The Chief Inspector awaits, silent and still. I step forward and offer the device. It is accepted, and as it's placed on a floating plinth, I watch with fascination as a new key materializes in the air: tarnished silver, slightly larger than the first. It falls into my hand with a satisfying weight.

Two keys now. One more to go.

I'm writing this down in a quiet alcove near the Office's edge. My heart is still racing, my mind buzzing with questions, but I have a sense of momentum now. I'm doing what they ask, and they're granting me the keys. After one more case, if I'm lucky, I can negotiate my release. I can go home.

I must not lose hope. I've come this far, and I won't stop now.

(Entry #5: A Final Assignment—The Endless Hotel)

The second key rests heavy in my pocket, proof that I can bend these places to my will—or at least survive their trials. I stand in the Office's central chamber once more, leaning against a low table that wasn't there a moment ago, trying to steady my breathing. Two keys earned, one yet to go. The Chief Inspector lingers somewhere in the background of my vision, neither approaching nor retreating. I can feel their attention as a prickling at the nape of my neck.

I steel myself and speak into the hush, my voice surprisingly steady. "The next assignment. Give it to me."

No direct reply. Instead, a door that wasn't there before swings inward without a creak, revealing a corridor lit by a warm glow. From inside that passage comes a piece of delicate, chiming music—like old lounge tunes playing far away down a long hallway. I approach, hesitant yet determined, and find a single slip of paper tacked to the doorway. On it, in neat ink, are just a few words:

Case #3: Recover the lost artifact that maintains the bridge between worlds.

Vague, but by now I'm used to it. I know that the ledger will have more. Sure enough, flipping it open, I find a sketch: an impossibly tall hotel, ornate and old-fashioned, with countless floors drawn one atop another. Arrows indicate lifts that move silently between levels and a note in the margin reads: *The artifact lies in a room that doesn't exist on any known floor. Look for signs of subtle differences. Trust no map but your instincts.* I run my finger over the ink, feeling a strange static crackle. This final task will not be straightforward.

"After this," I say to nobody in particular, "I get to go home." It's a promise I whisper into the still air.

I follow the corridor into a space that widens gradually until it resembles the lobby of a grand hotel: polished floors that reflect a hazy chandelier's glow, a reception desk empty of staff, and potted plants whose leaves are too symmetrical, too perfect. The air smells faintly of lemon polish and old velvet upholstery. Straight ahead, an elevator with brass doors waits silently, its indicator needle trembling between floors with no numbers.

I step across the lobby, my footsteps muted. No front desk clerk appears. No guests come or go. But I sense presences in the periphery: shapes behind frosted glass doors, distant murmurs behind closed paneling. The ledger said I must find a room that doesn't exist. How does one do that? By searching for anomalies, I suppose—the same way I freed the traveler and retrieved the device.

A stand near the elevator holds old brochures, each describing the hotel's amenities. One brochure reads: *"At the Grand Ascent Hotel, every floor is a world unto itself."* Another lists floor numbers—100, 200, 300—and their attractions: tea salons, reading rooms, observation decks. The numbers mean nothing to me, but I commit them to memory, searching for something that stands out. One page shows a floor plan that repeats itself infinitely: rooms numbered 1 through 998, and then... blank space. No mention of room 999. That's my clue. The artifact must be in a room that no official record includes.

I step into the elevator and press a button that bears no number, just a faint symbol like interlocking loops. The doors hush closed and I feel a gentle lift, as if the cabin moves upward. The ride is silent, without mechanical sounds. After what might be minutes, the doors open on a corridor lined with deep burgundy carpet and lamps that cast a warm, golden light. I walk, peering at room numbers: 901, 902, 903... up and up they go as I explore other floors. I ride the elevator again and again, stopping at different levels, and scanning room numbers. They always end at 998. Then it loops. 1, 2, 3... 901... 997, 998. No sign of 999.

This is a riddle: how to reach a room that "doesn't exist"? The ledger's pages show me nothing new. I recall how I manipulated the mirror corridor by turning my flashlight off and counting. In the second case, I used a whispered phrase and the keys I possessed. Perhaps now I must do something similar. I have two keys—obsidian dark and tarnished silver—and I carry them together in one hand, feeling their subtle warmth. They pulse faintly, as if alive with stored potential.

At another stop, I step out into a corridor that looks nearly identical to the last. The painting on the wall—an old landscape of a misty forest—catches my eye. On previous floors, the painting's forest scene was slightly different: sometimes a deer stood among the trees, sometimes not. Here, there's a faint glow in the distance behind the pines that I don't recall seeing before. This might be the subtle difference I need.

I open the ledger and tilt it so the chandelier's light falls across the page. My breath fogs slightly as if the air cooled. The page now shows a faint inscription: *To find the room beyond numbering, do what cannot be done. Ask the lift to pass its limit, and reflect on who you are.* Another puzzle. I must "ask" the lift to go beyond its known floors.

Back to the elevator, I go. Inside, I hold up my keys and speak to the empty air: "I need room 999." My voice wavers slightly. The lift's indicator trembles. I try a different approach. I press all the buttons at once, but they vanish beneath my fingertips, leaving a smooth brass panel. I flick off my flashlight, count to ten as before, then turn it on again. The buttons reappear, jumbled. One button now shows the number 999 faintly scratched into its surface.

I press it without hesitation. The elevator drops or rises—I can't tell which—my stomach lurching. The doors open onto a corridor that feels... off. The lamps flicker, the carpet pattern is reversed, and the door numbers show impossible sequences: 994, 995, 996, 997, 998... and then a gap on the wall where a door should be just blank wallpaper.

I approach the blank space. If this is where room 999 should be, how do I open it? I try pressing my palm flat against the wallpaper. It feels slightly elastic, giving under my touch. I take out my keys and press them to the wall. A low hum resonates through the corridor. The wallpaper distorts, shimmering like a heat haze, revealing a faint outline of a door. The knob materializes under my hand, a cool brass shape that shouldn't exist.

I turn the knob and step through.

The room beyond is small and dim, lit by a single lamp on a round table. The table holds an artifact: a crystalline shard, the size of my palm, glowing softly from within as if capturing starlight. I know instinctively this is what I've been sent to find. The artifact resonates with my heartbeat, each pulse sending shards of light dancing around the walls.

I reach out and pick it up. It's weightless, yet I feel its importance. This must be what maintains bridges between worlds. Without it, these realms could fracture. With it, perhaps the Inspector will have no choice but to let me go.

As I hold the shard, something stirs behind me: a presence, a whisper of breath against the back of my neck. I turn, startled. A form stands there—my shape reflected at me, but the face is blank. In a voice exactly like mine, it asks: "Who are you when no one watches?"

A test. I realize the question is not just philosophical. If I can't assert my identity, I might never leave this place. I steel myself: "I am a detective. I am human. I come from a city with rain-slick streets and coffee shops, from a life with rules and gravity, where I had a name." I say my name out loud, something I haven't done since arriving here, and it warms my tongue like a memory of hearthfire. "I know who I am, and I want to go home."

The figure tilts its head and then dissolves into smoke. The room's door now stands open behind me. Cradling the artifact, I step back into the corridor. The door fades away, leaving only blank wallpaper. I return to the lift, insert the two keys into slots that appear momentarily on its panel, and watch as the elevator whisks me away without me pressing a thing.

Moments later, I'm back in the Office lobby. The Chief Inspector awaits. I approach, holding the artifact high. They seem pleased—if "pleased" can be attributed to a formless silhouette. The artifact floats from my hand onto a waiting stand. The air crackles. My keys, along with the artifact, emit a glow. And then, with a soft pop, a third key forms, this one brighter, lighter, shimmering like polished crystal.

I have my three keys now. I'm writing this down, heart thudding, my mind full of questions. The final negotiation awaits. I must barter my keys and the artifact's return for my freedom. After everything I've endured, they must let me go. I'll speak to them next, holding my ground, insisting on the bargain we made without words.

I must return home. I won't settle for anything less.

(Entry #6: The Final Bargain and the Way Home)

The three keys rest heavily in my pocket—obsidian dark, tarnished silver, and now this crystalline one that gleams like a captured shard of moonlight. I clutch them together, feeling their subtle warmth, and I know this must be the moment of truth. The artifact I recovered—the luminous shard that helps maintain these fractured realms—floats serenely on a pedestal conjured out of nowhere as if both highly valued and casually displayed.

I stand in the Office's central space again. The atmosphere is charged as if the very air is holding its breath. The Chief Inspector waits, a silhouette of shifting density at the far end of the room. They have not spoken aloud to me once, not in any language I recognize, yet we've communicated through symbols, gestures, and these strange exchanges of objects and tasks. Now, I feel their regard like a weight against my chest.

I produce the keys from my pocket and hold them out, my voice calm but resolute. "I've done what you asked. Three cases, three keys. I have the artifact here, returned safely. You promised—at least, it was implied—that I'd be allowed to go home."

A silence follows. I'm used to this silence now, and yet it still unnerves me. I press on, taking a step forward. "I'm no prisoner. I've upheld my end of the bargain. Without my help, who would have freed that traveler, retrieved the stabilizer, and recovered this artifact? Let me go. Show me the way back to my city, my life."

For a moment, the Office flickers. The furniture subtly rearranges itself: a chair scrapes across the floor without a sound, and a lamp tilts on its base. Something about this place seems to strain as if the fabric of these halls is thinning. I sense that the Inspector wields the authority to end my journey here—or deny it. My pulse pounds, but I don't look away.

At last, the Inspector lifts a hand-shaped darkness toward me. Though I cannot see their face, I feel scrutiny, as if they are weighing my identity, my worth. This is it, I think. The final judgment. If they refuse, I'll break something, smash the artifact, or tear the pages from the ledger. I've come too far to be denied.

In response to my silent threat, a ripple passes through the air. The Inspector inclines their head. I take it as acquiescence. The corridor behind them bends and twists, the walls warping until a shimmering doorway appears. Its surface ripples like water in the moonlight, and beyond it, I think I see familiar shapes: the outline of my apartment's hallway, the bookshelf, the coat rack...

A lump forms in my throat. I didn't realize how much I craved the mere sight of my home until now. My legs want to sprint forward, but I hold steady, waiting. I must be sure this isn't another illusion.

The Inspector raises a hand again. In the hush, I think I hear their voice at last—just a whisper, a thin thread of meaning sliding into my mind. *You have done well. Return, if you choose. You will not be forgotten.* It's not a language of words, but intent and emotion, carried by the silence itself. I believe I understand: they are granting me passage, and also leaving the door open, in a sense, should I ever stray back into these realms.

"I'm going home," I say. "Thank you. Or goodbye. Or both."

No reply, just a subtle nod. I feel no triumph, only relief. This place has tested me and changed me. I don't know if it's good or bad, but I know I must leave now before I lose my resolve. Clutching the keys tight, I approach the shimmering doorway. The artifact and its pedestal remain behind, ensuring that these corridors will continue to exist for others who pass through, for better or worse.

As I step through, the air chills for a moment, then warms abruptly. My vision blurs, and I lurch forward, nearly stumbling. Instead of silent halls and shifting offices, I see the familiar shape of my apartment's front door just a foot away. The thin morning light slants through my window blinds. Everything smells right—coffee grounds on the kitchen counter, the faint scent of laundry detergent. My watch reads the same time and date it did when I first chased Marina into that abandoned building. It's as if no time has passed at all.

I slam the door closed behind me, pressing my back against it. My heart pounds. I'm back. I flick on the kitchen light. It hums comfortingly. I open the fridge—still half a carton of milk, still last night's leftovers. Everything is in place, except for the keys in my pocket and the notebook in my hand. These things don't belong here, proof that I wasn't just dreaming.

I settle at my small kitchen table, the one I remember seeing as a mirage back in those corridors. The diary, this notebook I've been writing in, sits before me. I run my hand over its cover. Every word I wrote, every surreal experience, is recorded here. I half-expect the pages to have gone blank, but they remain full of my cramped handwriting.

I consider calling Marina's brother, telling him what I've found—or rather, what I haven't found. I never found Marina. Did I fail my original case, or did I step out of that world line entirely? The thought is unsettling. Yet, for now, I'm safe, anchored in my reality. Maybe Marina was never in that building. Maybe her disappearance was a thread leading me astray, into something else entirely. I can't say. I will have to live with that uncertainty.

I leave the three keys on the table, examining them under the kitchen light. Their material is like nothing I've seen, not metal, not stone. Each one represents a solved case, a completed trial. They are useless here, I suspect. The portal they opened is gone—unless I stumble through such a doorway again. A chill runs down my spine. Once is enough. I think I'll avoid strange corridors and abandoned buildings from now on.

I write this final entry, my hand steady, my mind weary but clear. I need the record if only to remind myself that it happened. Without these pages, I might convince myself it was all a fever dream. But no—these keys are cold and real in my hand. The memory of endless corridors, odd clients, shifting reflections, and impossible hotels is too vivid to forget.

In the end, I have changed. I feel older, wiser, and sadder. I've learned that the boundaries of our world are thinner than we think and that there are cracks through which one can slip. I'll return to normal detective work—there are still missing people and unanswered questions in my city. But I'll always keep an eye on doorways, watch for subtle changes in familiar rooms, and listen for distant hums that shouldn't be there.

I close the diary and lock it away in my desk drawer. Outside, the city hums on as usual. Cars roll past, and distant sirens rise and fade. It's reassuringly mundane. The smell of my old life surrounds me, and I breathe it in like a healing balm.

(Later, A Brief Note)

Just now, I found something odd tucked into the pocket of my coat: a business card, dark ink on thick paper. The same sigil I saw in the Office is printed there—no address, no name, just a symbol that makes my pulse quicken. I should throw it away, but I can't quite bring myself to. Instead, I slip it back into the drawer with the diary and the keys.

I'm free now—back where I belong. But the memory of those impossible halls will never leave me. Perhaps that's the cost of touching a greater mystery: you carry a piece of it with you forever. I'm willing to bear that weight, grateful that I still know who I am, still know my name, and still have a place to call home.

I'll set down my pen. My story in those other worlds is done, at least for now. I'm a detective in my city once more, no longer a stranger caught between spaces. That's all I've ever wanted. That's enough.

Also by TheWizardCow

Winter Hygge Coloring Book

✧ **Embrace the enchanting spirit of winter coziness** with this heartwarming collection of hand-drawn illustrations that capture the essence of hygge! ✧

Scary Horror Stories Collection

When the clock strikes a moment beyond midnight, reality splinters, and the world gives way to its hidden horrors. **Scary Horror Stories Collection** invites you to step into the darkened realms where echoes whisper, shadows come alive, and nothing is ever what it seems.